Philomel
An imprint of Penguin Random House LLC, New York

First published in the United States of America by Philomel,
an imprint of Penguin Random House LLC, 2024

Philomel is a registered trademark of Penguin Random House LLC.
The Penguin colophon is a registered trademark of Penguin Books Limited.

Visit us online at PenguinRandomHouse.com.

Library of Congress Cataloging-in-Publication Data is available.

ISBN 9780593624333

10 9 8 7 6 5 4 3 2 1

Manufactured in China

HH

Edited by Jill Santopolo
Design by Rory Jeffers

Text set in Mercury.
Art was created with gouache, ink, colored pencil, and crayon.

The publisher does not have any control over and does not assume
any responsibility for author or third-party websites or their content.

HAPPY ST. PATRICK'S DAY
FROM THE CRAYONS

PHILOMEL

It's St. Patrick's Day and Green
Crayon is on vacation! Uh-oh!
What will Duncan do?

Don't worry, Duncan.

We gotchoo.

Mm-hmm

PURPLE

WHITE

The other crayons decide to help.

It'll be an extraordinary collaboration!

Blue and Yellow colored
the field of shamrocks—together.

But it was a lot of work.

So White colored the leprechaun's underwear.

YOU can't FORGET the Leprechaun's UNDERWEAR! YOU gotta WEAR UNDERWEAR! Sheesh!

WHITE

Orange colored
the pants.

Pink colored the leprechaun's vest.

Purple colored the leprechaun's coat and boots.

Chunky Toddler Crayon
did the hat.

Then there was that harp.

Now that everything was ready,
there was just one thing left to do . . .
party!

HAPPY ST.

ORANGE

WHITE

PATRICK'S DAY !!